WORST. MISSION. EVER.

Join Pirate Blunderbeard on more adventures:

Pirate Blunderbeard
WORST. PIRATE. EVER.

Pirate Blunderbeard
WORST. HOLIDAY. EVER.

Pirate Blunderbeard
WORST. MISSION. EVER.

Coming Soon

Pirate Blunderbeard
WORST. MOVIE. EVER.

WORST. MISSION. EVER.

AMY SPARKES & BEN CORT

HarperCollins *Children's Books*

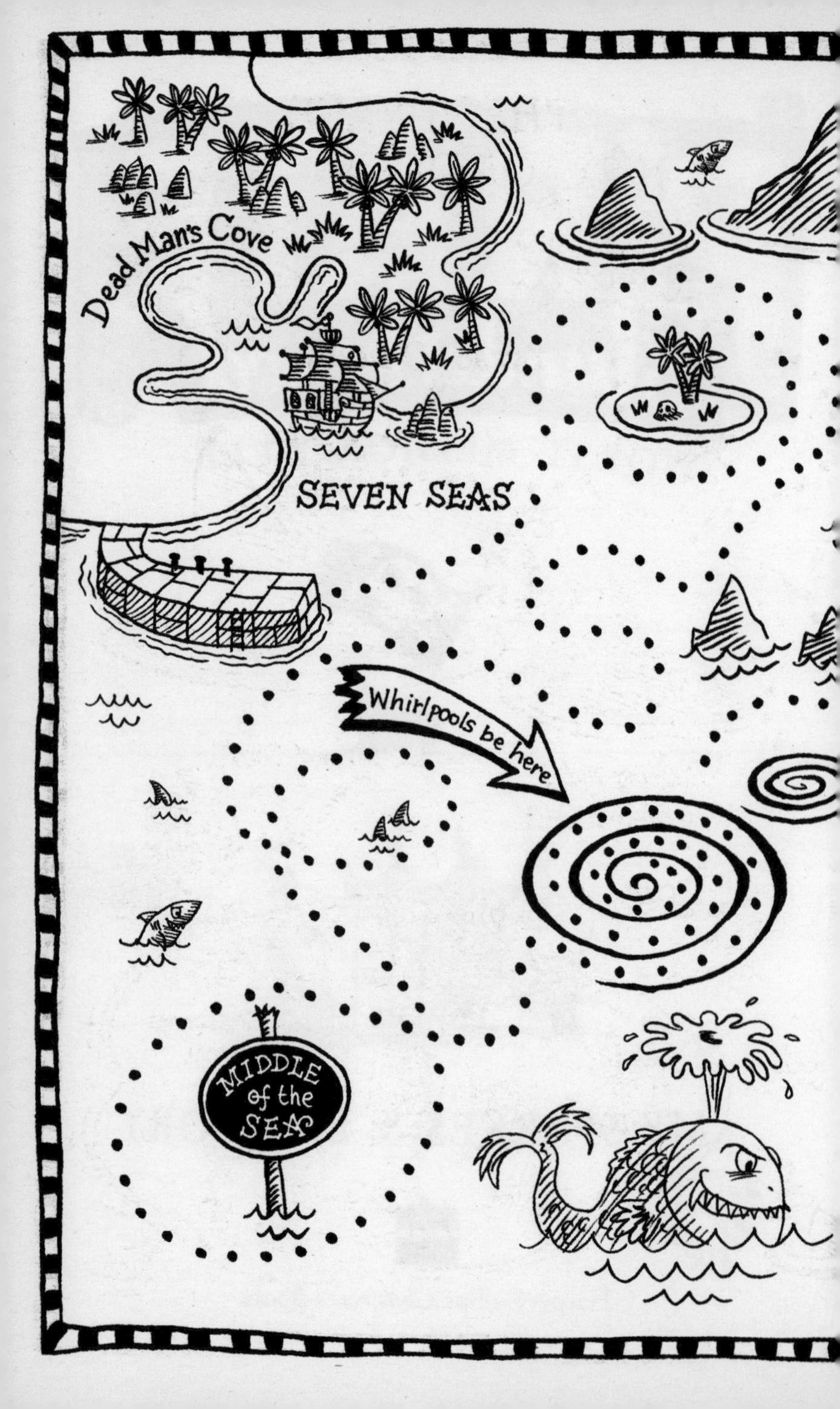
Dead Man's Cove
SEVEN SEAS
Whirlpools be here
MIDDLE of the SEA

THE VOYAGE OF DOOM
Breath O'Death
Laughing Skull
Pirating Today
Newspaper HQ
Port Savage
Skull and Crossbones
Restaurant
DOOM ISLAND

Mum
Blackbeard
Blunderbeard
Dread Pirate Madlocks
Lazy Jim
Boris

Uncle Redbeard

Redruth

Captain Chomp

Grandad Greybeard

First published in Great Britain by HarperCollins *Children's Books* in 2018
HarperCollins *Children's Books* is a division of HarperCollins*Publishers* Ltd,
HarperCollins *Publishers*,1 London Bridge Street, London, SE1 9GF

The HarperCollins website address is:
www.harpercollins.co.uk

1

ISBN 978-0-00-820190-6

Typeset in Bembo Schoolbook 15pt/26pt
Printed and bound by CPI Group (UK) Ltd, Croydon, CR0 4YY

MIX
Paper from
responsible sources
FSC™ C007454

This book is produced from independently certified FSC™ paper to ensure responsible forest management.

For more information visit: www.harpercollins.co.uk/green

For Alex and Izzy
And for the real GG – with thanks
for all the adventures x

Amy Sparkes is donating a percentage of
her royalties to ICP Support, aiming for
every ICP baby to be born safely.

Reg. charity no. 1146449
www.icpsupport.org

Heading off with Grandpa Greybeard and Cousin Redruth to sail the Seven Seas!

Hurrah!

We'll be out on the waves … Sun on my face … Salt in the air …

We can set up the deckchairs and have ice creams. Mmm, mint chocolate for me! Think I've got some Chick-O-Snacks-flavoured lollies in the freezer for Boris.

Maybe we'll stop off at interesting places. Ooh – I could get a new pirate hat for me and a bucket and spade for Boris.

Here are my New Year's resolutions:

1. Stop biting nails –
   THIS TIME I **WILL** DO THIS.

2. Teach Boris how to be a homing chicken. (She could take postcards to my brother Blackbeard – he'll be so jealous when he reads about our travels. Haha.)

3. Survive an adventure with Redruth and Grandpa Greybeard. I hope.

This … is going to be **great!**

Or not.

Grandpa has written these New Year's resolutions in MY diary by mistake!!!

1. *Teach the lily-livered kids a thing or two about pirating!*
2. *Face death and danger on the Seven Seas (and be back in time for me evening rum)!*
3. *Risk life and limb and settle me "business" with THE BOSS once and for all.*

What in the name of Neptune's nasal hair does THAT mean?! Probably that I'm in for a year of adventure and disaster – with as much chance of reaching December in one piece as Boris has of being a world-famous limbo dancer …

We dropped anchor in the middle of the sea.

Then I dropped Boris in the middle of the sea.

All because Redruth crept up behind me and blasted her PortaCannon™ while

Boris and I were looking out for boats selling ice cream.

So, nope.

Not my fault at all.

Boris reckons it's my fault.

Grandpa hasn't said *why* we've stopped. Just that he's got a plan.

OK ... A plan. Sounds ... interesting.

Except "interesting" in my life is not usually good.

6.30am

AAAARGH!! Grandpa just woke me up by dumping a bucket of cold, rotten fish over me and shouting:

"Wake up, ye lazy, lily-livered limpet! It be Day One of Proper Pirate Training! HAARRRRRRR!"

Blargh!!! Just spat a rotten fish-tail out of my mouth. It be Proper What?!

Grandpa has gone off dancing a hornpipe and humming a sea shanty.

Not good.

6.30pm

Ouch. Sword. Fight.

Hours. And. Hours.

Redruth. Fit. Me. Not.

Arm. Ache. Shattered.

Bed. Argh. Forgot.

Rotten. Fish. Yuck. Bed.

Squelch.

6.30am

AAAARGH!!

Rotten fish on face.

"Wake up, ye dozy dogfish! It be Day Two of Proper Pirate Training!"

Oh. Please. NO!!!!!

6.30pm

Rigging. Climbing. Hate. Heights. Fell. Lots. Water. Wet. Totally. Shattered. Bed.

Argh.

Fish.

6.30am

Slept with umbrella over face.

Rotten fish.

"Get up, ye sluggish sea cucumber! It be Day Three of training.

6.30pm

Pretending. Capture. Ships. All. Day.

Squelch. Really. Should. Clean. Bed. Now.

6.30am

Day Nine.

Rotten fish.

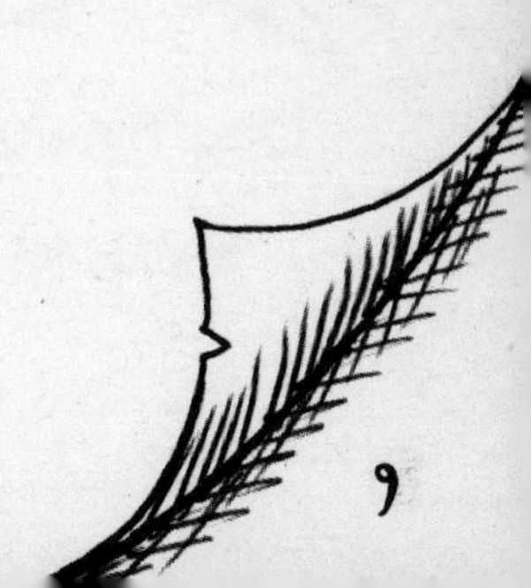

Please, for the love of cupcakes, someone make this awful training stop!

WHAT'S IT FOR ANYWAY??!!!!

6.30am

Day Seventeen.

Rotten tomatoes.

Grandpa's run out of rotten fish.

He keeps dancing the hornpipe and muttering, "We'll show the Boss."

Day Twenty-eight.

SAVE ME. ☹

8am

Overslept.

Overslept?!

No rotten food on the face today?! Training's finally over?

All quiet (except for Boris snoring).

What's going on?

4pm

Grandpa just called me and Redruth up on to the deck and explained everything. He was jiggling about as if he had an electric eel in his trousers.

And clapping his hands, all excited.

"HAHARRR!" he boomed. "Me hearties, we be off to meet our fate!"

Redruth said, "Totally excellent," at the same time as I said, "Fate?! OUR?!"

Turns out "the dreaded Boss" is the

nickname of the scariest pirate on the seas. And that's coming from Grandpa. His real name is Dread Pirate Madlocks and a few years ago he stole Grandpa's ship and made him walk the plank. That's how Grandpa got stranded on the Island of No Return (although he was a bit embarrassed about it all and spread rumours that his ship had gone down in a storm).

Now Grandpa has left the Island of No Return, he wants his old ship back. And he thinks Redruth and I are just the pirates to help him ... Yes, we're on a mission to steal a ship from THE SCARIEST PIRATE ON THE SEAS.

If I may say just one thing? ...

HEEEEEEELP!
HEEEEEEELP!

Why do I get the feeling we are heading for big,

BIG,

BIG,

BIG trouble?

Oh dear. Oh very dear.

Redruth just showed me Pirate Madlocks in the "Who's Who" section of her *Pirate Monthly* magazine.

HEEEEEEEELP!
HEEEEEEELP!

WHO'S WHO ON THE SEVEN SEAS

This month: Pirate Madlocks

Hangs out: Somewhere/anywhere on the Seven Seas, nicking your ship

Likes: Ship-stealing, bone-breaking, sword-fighting

Dislikes: Idiots, pesky little pirates

Awards won include:

- *Pirates United Swordfighters* (PUS): **Best Swordfighter** every year since the award started. (He fights anyone who asks him to hand the trophy back so they decided it was safer to just let him keep it.) Barber Rossa's **Craziest Hair of the Year Award**.

- *Pirate Monthly*'s **Scariest Pirate Who We Are Seriously Impressed With Award.** Twice.

Pirate Pet: Vicious sea-dog called Whoopsie.

***Pirate Monthly's* Awesomely Dangerous Pirate Rating:** 10/10

Dislikes idiots? And pesky little pirates?! GULP.

Grandpa came and joined us on deck and sang this sea shanty:

"The dreaded Boss, he rules the seas,
Heave ho, me crazy crew,
Ye'll be a-crawling on yer knees,
Heave ho, good luck to you!

The oceans roared, the cannons boomed,
Heave ho, me crazy crew,
Now we're stuffed and really doomed.
Heave ho, good luck to you!"

Marvellous.

We are sailing full speed ahead to our certain doom. (Although I'm sure Grandpa doesn't quite know where he's going and no one else seems at all worried! This. Is. Not. Good.)

OK … I hate having to do this. But I'm going to contact *The Pirates Against Rubbish Piracy Society* (PARPS). Surely they'll have to do something about a pirate putting his crew in danger? Maybe they'll stop this VOYAGE OF DOOM or whatever it is, rescue me and then I can just go home and bake some cakes in peace?!

Boris can take the message. I'll just train

her as a homing chicken. I KNEW that resolution would come in handy.

What can possibly go wrong?

OK … LOTS.

More later when I've put out the fire. And cleaned cupcakes off the cabin ceiling.

And got Boris's head unstuck from the teapot.

Took Boris up on deck, sat her on my shoulder, then let her fly free!

Thought she might fly around over the sea for a couple of minutes, then come back.

She's now sitting up in the crow's nest and refusing to come down.

Oh. That. Chicken!! How many pirates in the history of EVER have had to stand at the bottom of the mast pleading with a chicken?! ☹

Redruth laughed for an hour.

Forget the whole thing. I'm sending PARPS a message in a bottle.

I need to get out of this VOYAGE OF DOOM as soon as possible!

9am

So the only bottle I could find was this: Boris's medicine – *that makes bunged-up chickens poo!!* How embarrassing does my life have to be??

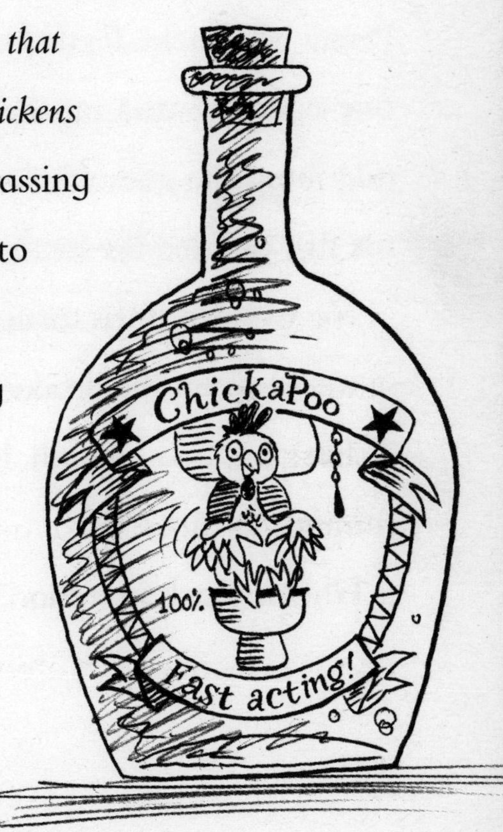

I was just trying to decide what to do with the liquid inside the bottle when

Redruth walked in and asked what it was. NO WAY was I telling her that it was "the leading brand of constipation medicine for today's stressed-out chicken". I told her it was a vitamin drink I'm taking so that I'll be on top form when we meet Dread Pirate Madlocks. Redruth did that raise-one-eyebrow-and-put-her-head-on-one-side thing she does when she doesn't believe me so I guzzled the lot. In one go.

No wonder Boris turns the colour of seaweed when she drinks it!! YUCK! And if that's not bad enough, I have to keep running to the—

Uh-oh. Back in a mo.

9.30am

Where was I? Oh yeah. I have to keep running to the—

Hang on.

9.50am

To the—

10.15am

I—

10.30am

Hate—

10.45am

Redruth.

3pm

Phew. Oh, my tummy! Think I'm OK now.

I can't BELIEVE I'm writing to PARPS using a bottle that helps chickens poo ☹. But I need them to rescue us from this doomed mission. Maybe they won't notice …

The Breath O'Death
I Have No Idea Where
The Ocean
April 21st

Dear PARPS,

When I wrote to you last year, it is possible I may have been a teensy bit rude. To be fair, you had stranded me on the awful Island of No Return, and I was feeling smug as I'd just rescued myself by getting a lift with Grandpa Greybeard...

However, it turns out I'm in a little spot of bother. Grandpa is very excited. He's taking us on a mission to get his ship back. On this mission he reckons we will "meet our fate" – a fate of the "stuffed and really doomed" type. This is his idea of FUN!! Surely, he can't be allowed to put his crew in danger?? This must count as rubbish pirating? Please???? So I should be allowed to leave the mission, right? Like, now??

Very much hoping you might come and sort of rescue me, before the whole "stuffed and doomed" bit.

Yours, more respectfully,

Barnacles Blunderbeard

Inventor, Senior Tester,

Chief Executive, Baker

Blunderbeard's WonderWeird Contraptions

I can see Blackbeard's parrot, Ironclaw! He's coming this way! He's bringing a message in his beak! I'm saved! I'm saved! I'm—

Argh!

He pooped in my eye.

Fiendish beast!!

May your beak go blunt!!

Opening letter now. Yay! When are they coming to rescue me?

Pirates Against Rubbish Piracy Society

The Best Pirate Ship in the World

Dead Man's Cove

The Ocean

April 28th

Dear Blunderbeard,

Hahahahahahaha!!!!!! No chance.

Enjoy "meeting your fate".

Yours sincerely,

Blasterous Blackbeard

(Director of PARPS)

P.S. I can't believe you actually used a bottle of chicken poo medicine to contact us! It took ages to reach us. Haven't you heard of homing parrots?? Pirates haven't used bottles for about one hundred years! PARPS feel that your old-fashioned and insulting action (chicken poo??!!) is simply unacceptable and that this is another example of YOUR rubbish pirating. Just because you've gone off with Grandpa Greybeard, don't think you're a proper pirate now. You're not, Blunderbeard. Proper pirates DON'T NEED RESCUING!!! Idiot.

Ohhhh dear.

8am

Right. These are my options:

1) ~~Run away~~ (Redruth would find me).

2) ~~Boris and I lead a mutiny and take over the ship~~ (Redruth has her PortaCannon™ and she's a bit scary).

3) Try to get Grandpa's old ship back from Madlocks.

Poo.

Oh no! Boris! I didn't mean—! All over my diary! Oh. That. Chicken! I'll get a cloth. ☹

10am

Grandpa is cross because he still can't work out where Madlocks is at the moment.

I'm staying out of his way and working on homing chicken training for the completely useless Boris. Then she can take a letter to Mum and tell her about the trouble I'm in! Maybe Mum can help.

Blunderbeard's WonderWeird Contraptions are proud to present the …

HenHomer™

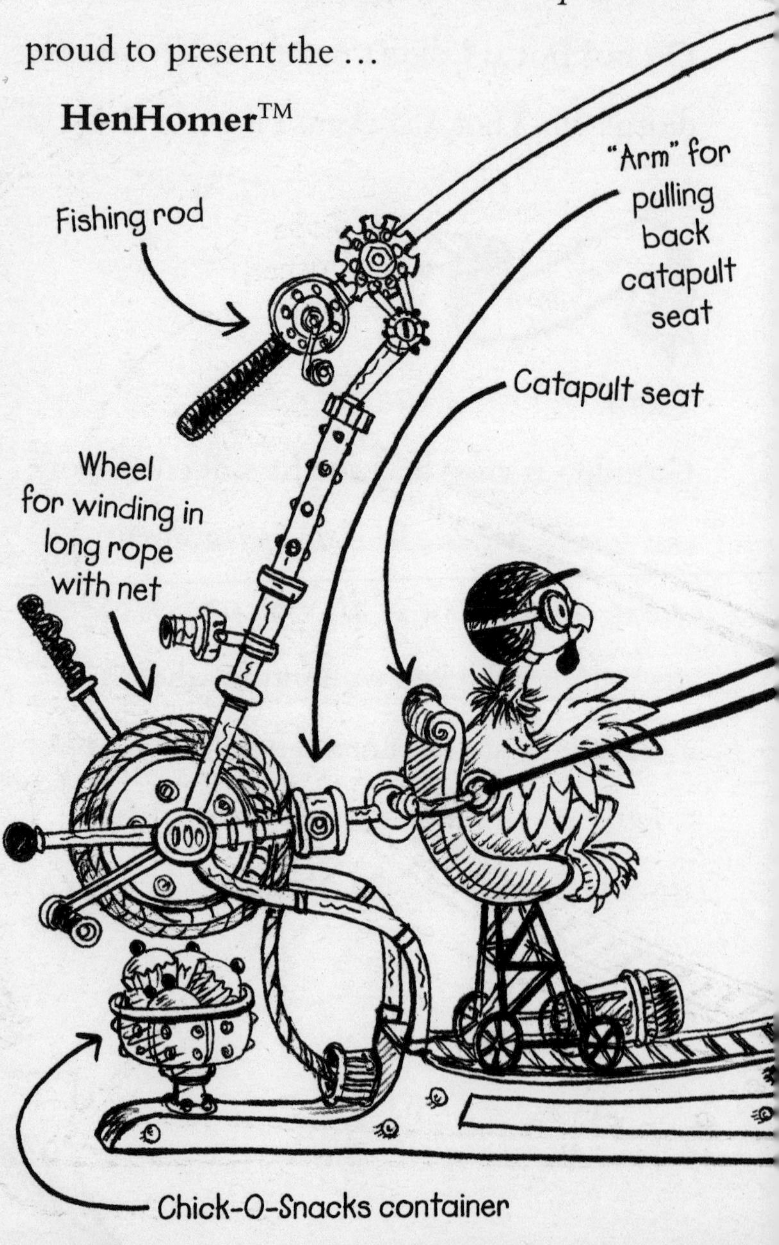

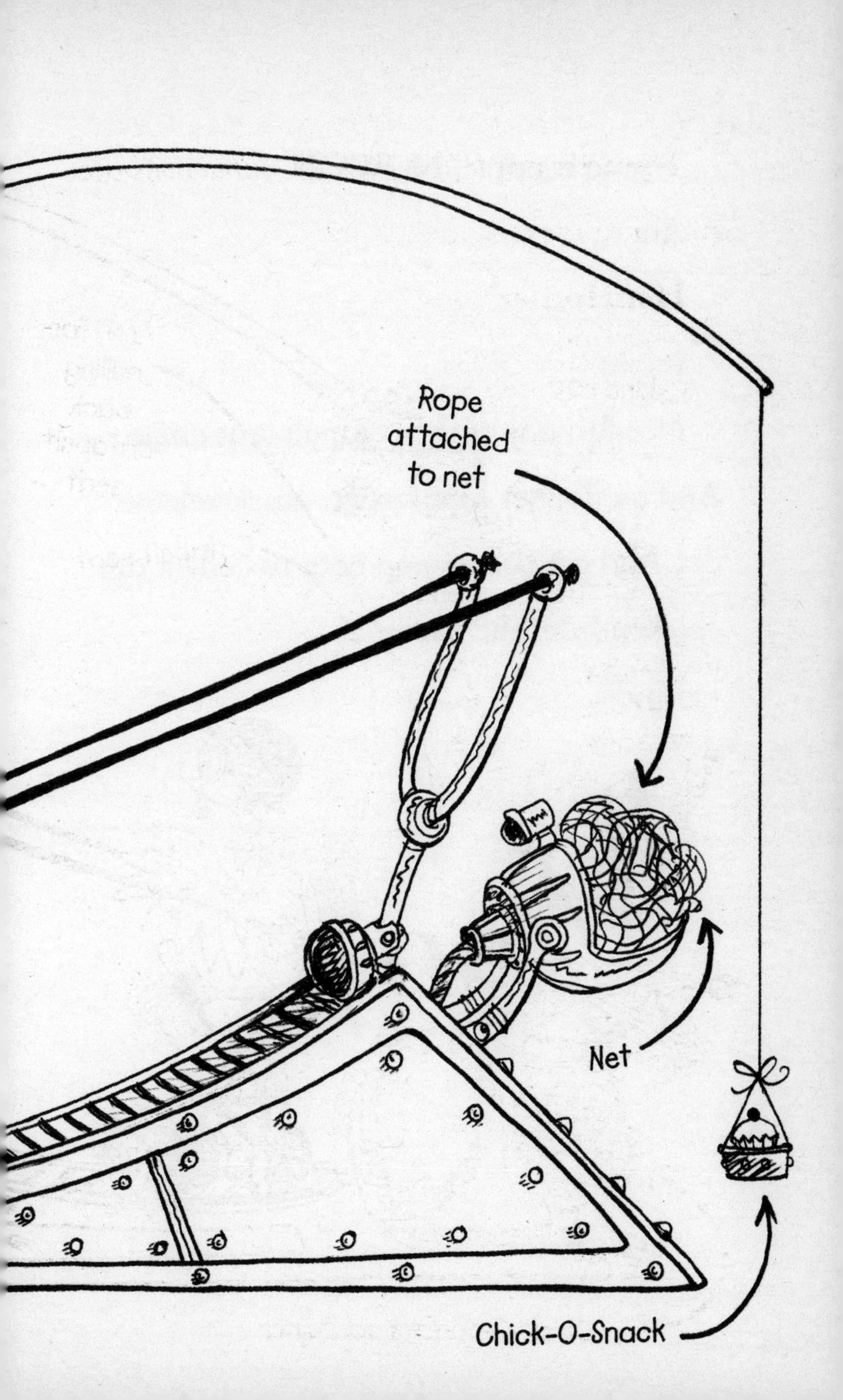
Rope
attached
to net
Net
Chick-O-Snack

Trying it out … NOW! ☺

Ah.

Um.

Right.

Need to adjust the catapult seat angle. And use longer rope on the quick-release net. And get the rowing boat to collect my chicken from the ocean …

Again.

Homing Chicken Training: Take Two.

She did it! She did it!!

I launched her into the sky, then cast out the fishing line with the cake attached. She did a neat spin in the air to try to catch the cake in her beak, then chased it back to the ship as I reeled in the line!

Success!! I have a genius for a chicken!!

Well … I have a chicken.

Boris is refusing to move. Apparently she's tired out after all her hard work training!

Humph! And I don't have any more bottles to send a message to Mum.

Only option left: being "stuffed and really doomed".

9am

Grandpa dancing the hornpipe and finishing with a double backflip. He's clutching a *Pirating Today* newspaper.

It says:

DREAD PIRATE MADLOCKS STRIKES AGAIN

The most amazing, fearsome pirate, Dread Pirate Madlocks, has recently taken eight ships in the Port Savage area of Doom Island. Unfortunately these include the office ship of *Pirating Today* (we're so proud – Madlocks is our hero), so there will be no more newspapers until next month.

9.30am

Heading to Doom Island (that sounds promising).

Grandpa has put me in charge of navigation.

I'm really chuffed. This is my chance to show him what a truly excellent, fabulous pirate I really am!

10.10am

WHIRLPOOL!

WE ARE

DOOMED!!!!!!

ABANDON

SHIP!

11.30am

Grandpa has put Redruth in charge of navigation.

I am now peeling potatoes for lunch. ☹

Not really my fault that the whirlpool appeared out of nowhere. Well, sort of nowhere. I suppose it did say "whirlpools be here" on my map. I just didn't realise we were on *that* bit of the map. Ahem.

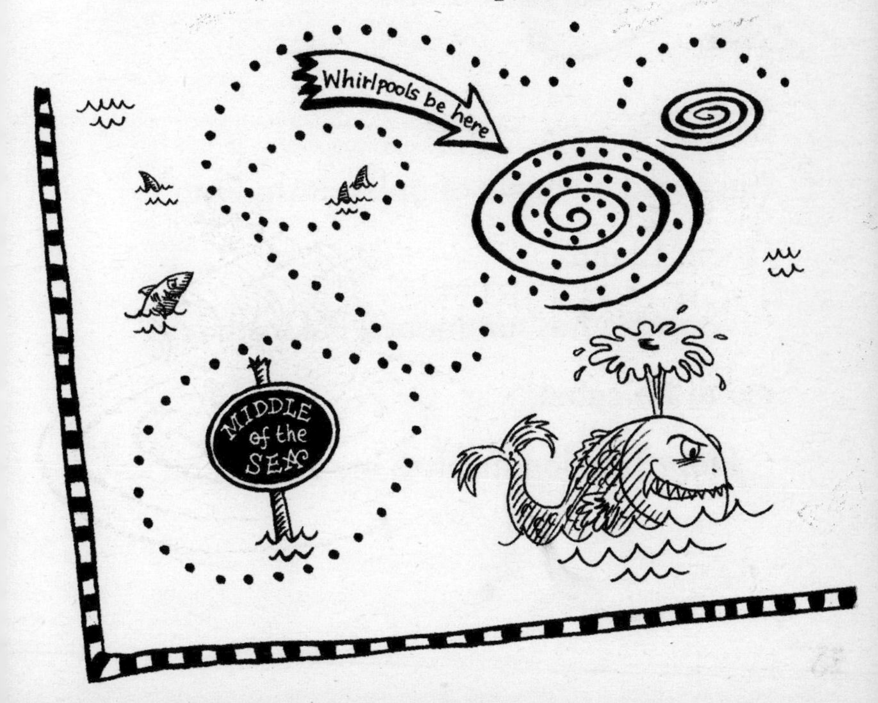

3pm

OK, we are NOW heading towards Doom Island. Grandpa still working on a plan. Can hear him muttering the words "hopeless" and "certain death" and "Blunderbeard". Not entirely sure this is a good sign. ☹

11.30am

Anchored a couple of miles away from Doom Island.

Grandpa has summoned Redruth and me to his cabin.

Hope his plan involves me staying on

board, inventing contraptions and baking cakes.

1pm

Nope. ☹

2pm

Grandpa looked through his telescope and saw Madlocks's boat anchored in Port Savage. He said he wished he could get a closer look. He reckons

Madlocks is such a fearsome pirate (even by Grandpa's standards) that we need to have the element of surprise. The only way we'll stand a chance is if he doesn't know we're here.

Back in cabin. Wish I could remember where I've heard Madlocks's name before. I'm sure it's important somehow ...

That's it!! That's IT! Even Redruth will have to admit I am a complete and utter genius! I have a brilliant idea!

The SpyChick™!!!

Now Boris has got the hang of the homing instinct, she can go and spy on the ship using a special camera and report back to me. I *knew* her training would come in handy.

Everyone's a winner: Boris gets to practise her homing, Grandpa gets useful information, I get to hide under my bed.

More later. Busy being a complete and utter genius. ☺

10am

Blunderbeard's WonderWeird Contraptions are proud to present:

The SpyChick™!

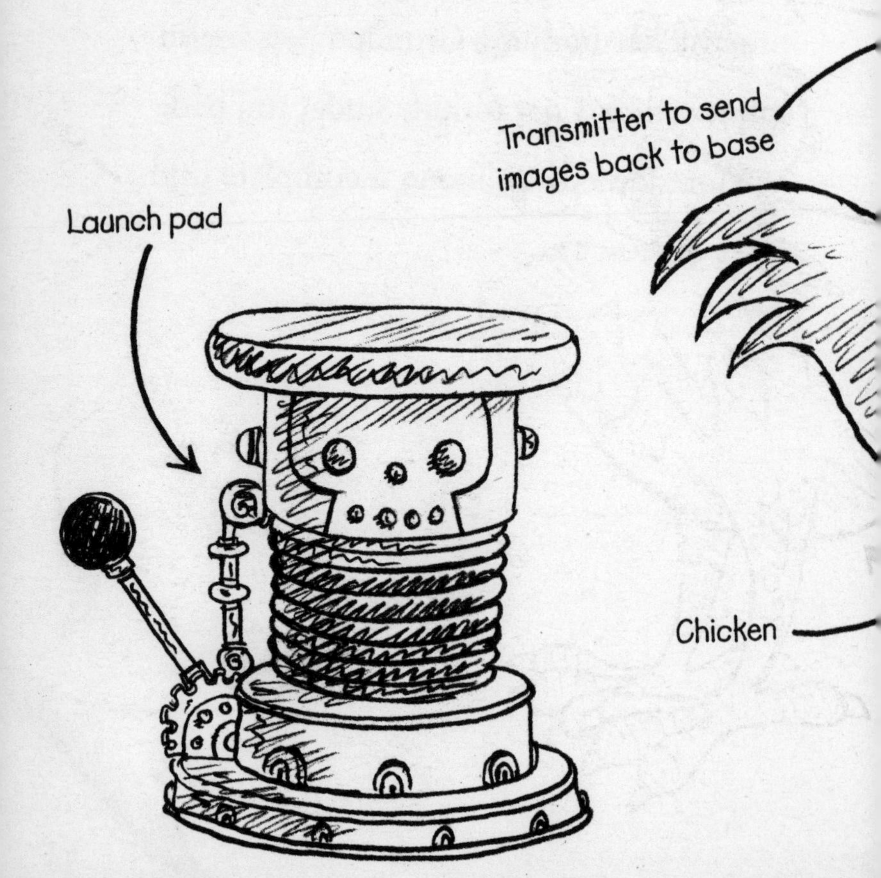

Video camera
Secret microphone
Chick-O-Snacks cupcake supply

Grandpa wasn't convinced by my plan. He grumbled on about "modern technology rubbish" and how, when he was a lad, they'd just storm a ship, take it over and be back in time for jelly and ice cream.

Redruth wasn't convinced either. She just wanted to sneak up, board the ship and blast all their hats off with her PortaCannon™.

But I've persuaded them to let me try the SpyChick™. It's a great idea. How can it possibly fail?

I'm making Redruth watch the screen with me so she can see my complete and utter genius-ness unfold before her very eyes. HA! That'll teach her.

11am

I've given "Boris the Bold" a quick ruffle of the feathers and am about to launch her.

3 … 2 … 1 … Chicks away!!

Wow. Look at her go. I'm so proud. So, SO proud.

We're watching on the screen. The plan is that she circles the boat a few times so we can look for any weaknesses that will help us capture it. Then she'll simply fly back to us undetected.

There we go … I can see Madlocks's ship on our screen. Wow. Lots of cannons. Swords. Gunpowder. Pirates. There's the vicious dog, Whoopsie, (oh – he's a poodle) and –

Oh no. She hasn't ... Tell me she hasn't ...

She's landed on the ship!!

Oh. That. Chicken!! She's just wandering around all over the place. Not even in a straight line!!

Oh no. Oh, Boris, no. PLEASE, NO.

She's gone to the ship's toilet!

But those boots ... they belong to *DREAD PIRATE MADLOCKS!*

She's gone into the toilet!! And – OOOOOH! Oh dear! I won't write down the words the microphone just picked up. To be fair, it must have come as a bit of a shock to Madlocks, a chicken wandering in when you're in the middle of having a – Wait! What has she just grabbed in her beak?

Oh no. Oh, Boris, no. NOT THE TOILET ROLL!

So *Pirate Monthly* gave Madlocks a 10/10 Awesomely Dangerous Pirate Rating. And my chicken has just run off with his toilet roll in her beak. LEAVING HIM STUCK ON THE TOILET!!!

I'm dead.

Microphone picking up Madlocks. He's bellowing for someone to get him some toilet paper RIGHT AWAY. Pirates everywhere, running around! And where's Boris going now??! She's flying up to the crow's nest! She's—

Oh no. Oh, Boris, no ... That's why she needed the toilet roll!

Right. No more ChickaPoo for Boris EVER AGAIN! ARGHH! Madlocks is furious! He's marching towards the crow's nest! With his trousers round his ankles! Oh no! Boris's poo – it's dripping on Madlocks's head!!

Argh!! The video camera battery has run out! Can hear Madlocks over the microphone. He says he's had enough. Six gold doubloons for the pirate who catches that "wretched bird" (yeek!) when they get back, but they've got to head off to the *Skull and Crossbones* at Port Savage now – they've booked a table for lunch at twelve o'clock to celebrate Madlocks winning Barber Rossa's Craziest Hair of the Year Award again. Can hear boots and doggy paws leaving the ship.

part from Boris … finishing off

ness". Hmm, wish the microphone

run out of battery now too.

Oh, for the love of cupcakes!!!!

Redruth laughed so much and said she was going to write to Mum and tell her all about it. In detail.

What do I do now??!! I can't leave Boris stuck on that ship, to be made into pie. ☹ And if Grandpa finds out what a disaster this is, he will go madder than Blackbeard did that time I put a crab in his pants.

I've got to rescue Boris, and I've got to do it now.

Well … I guess all the pirates are off the ship …

I could just *borrow* Grandpa's rowing boat again …

And hope I survive.

OH. THAT. CHICKEN!!!!

12pm

I want a parrot instead!!!!!!

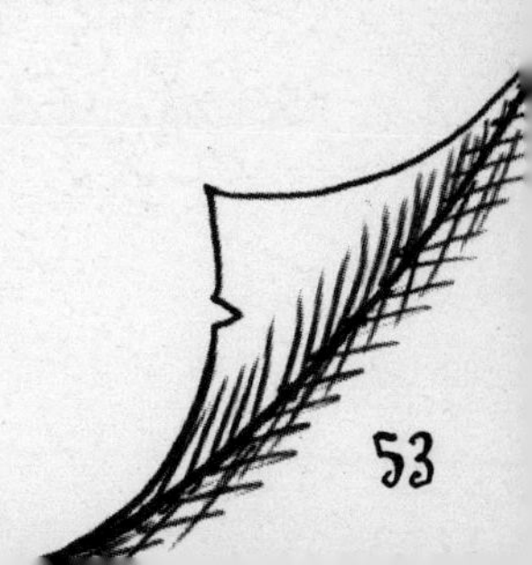

Left a note for Grandpa and Redruth explaining I've gone to rescue a rogue homing chicken and I might be late for supper (and don't let Redruth eat my pudding).

1pm

Pulled up the rowing boat beside Madlocks's ship. Can see Boris up in the crow's nest. No sign of pirates anywhere.

If I don't make it back, and this is my last entry, let it be known that brave young Blunderbeard perished on his quest to save his fearless, formerly constipated chicken, Boris the Bold, from being made into pie by the very fearsome

Dread Pirate Madlocks.

(Let it also be known that it was Redruth who nicked all the chocolate biscuits. Sorry, Grandpa, she swore me to secrecy.)

1.15pm

Am on board.

Has just occurred to me: I have done it! I, Blunderbeard, am on board Madlocks's ship! ME!!

Ha! I name myself CAPTAIN BARNACLES BLUNDERBEARD, Captain of the *Laughing Skull* (at least for a few minutes), with a *Pirate Monthly* Awesomely Dangerous Pirate Rating of

10/10! Brave explorer, expert sailor, rescuer of chickens in distress!

Hey, I've got a few minutes. Feel I should rescue Boris in style and try out some of my pirate training moves. Grandpa would be proud. And at least all those awful lessons won't have been for nothing.

I'll climb up some rigging, swing across to the main mast on that loose rope, then drop neatly into the crow's nest to grab Boris.

Here I go!!

OUCH.

That would be the main mast.

Climbing up into crow's nest …

ARGH!

Stepped right into a huge pile of chicken poo! Can't believe I forgot about that. ☹ Will take me ages to clean these boots. Oh well. Lucky there's some toilet paper left on the roll …

Going to grab Boris and swing back on the rope.

OUCH.

The other mast. OK, so ropes aren't my thing. Moving on . . .

1.19pm

Ooh, there's the captain's cabin. Dashing inside.

Any clues? Any weaknesses? Even a 10/10 pirate must have a weakness! If I can find it, Grandpa will be so proud of me.

Wait a minute! Look! *Captain Cook's Recipe Book: Volume 2: More Cakes*! I've got Volume One on Grandpa's ship. Not seen a Volume Two before. Madlocks must like his cakes, just like me. Ooh, this looks really good. Crunchy crab and raisin scones on page twenty-eight. Argh. Boris pulling at my sleeve with her beak. Get off! Daft chicken. Ooh: page thirty-three, seaweed sponge. Boris, stop it! She probably needs the toilet again, unless –

Uh-oh.

The sound of boots.

And tough, piratey voices.

HELP! We're going to be caught unless I think of a plan!!

1.21pm

Thought of a plan.

Boris and I are hiding in a large lidded basket in a corner of the cabin.

It was a brilliant plan. Until I realised this is Dread Pirate Madlocks's dirty laundry bin! The smell is AWFUL! And Boris keeps fidgeting next to me. Don't know *what* she's doing!! Ooh, look – Madlocks sews little nametags into his pants.

Removing the SpyChick™ equipment from Boris, just in case we get caught.

SSSSHHHH! Madlocks is coming in, with another pirate! Stuffed Boris's beak in a dirty sock to keep her quiet.

This is what they're saying:

"And you STILL haven't ordered some more special glue for my … well … for the *you-know-what.*"

"Sorry, Captain, Your Dreadfulness, Sir. I'll do it today. Your secret's safe with me."

"Better had be, Bones. Or you're walkin' the plank. And you don't want to be doin' that."

"Nay, Captain, Your Dreadfulness, Sir."

Gulp.

Guess we'll be waiting in here until he's gone, then. Surely he won't be long.

3.20pm

Still waiting.

So nervous am biting my nails again.

Really need a wee. ☹

And this laundry bin smells worse than Grandpa's aftershave.

4.20pm

Worried the sound of chewing fingernails is too noisy. Putting Madlocks's stinky socks on my hands to stop me biting nails.

GOOD GRIEF! Boris is actually wearing a pair of Madlocks's pants! How on the Seven Seas did she—? Never mind. At least Madlocks doesn't know about it. Don't think pirates like chickens wearing their pants. But we're safe. He has NO idea we're here—

Oh no. Oh very VERY no. Boris's beak is twitching. Her nostrils are smoking. We are DOOMED!! It's really not good when a chicken who is part-dragon lets out an enormous—

Oh. That. CHICKEN!!

Great. JUST GREAT.

Boris *bloomin'* Flamebeak SNEEZED.

The laundry bin whooshed up in the air and burst into flames.

The sock on her beak caught fire and went flying across the room.

The bin landed in a pile of ash.

We crashed in a heap at Madlocks's feet.

The fiery sock landed on a piece of paper Madlocks was holding.

It burned to a crisp.

As I looked up at him, trying to give him my best smile, I remembered that Boris was wearing his pants. And I was wearing his socks on my hands. Things were not going to go well.

His eyes went wide and he tugged his curls in rage and yelled "Toilet roll!"

several times and jumped up and down. Madlocks sent Boris to the kitchen. He's saving her to be made into chicken pie for his birthday meal. ☹

Madlocks asked me what a boy and a chicken were doing near his ship. I wouldn't tell him, but then he threatened to make me dance the hornpipe until dawn. So I just said I'd come from Grandpa's ship which was anchored nearby, and my chicken had flown off and got lost and I was trying to get her back (technically, all true). Then Madlocks held a "Sink Blunderbeard's Rowing Boat" competition with this crew. Then he sent his parrot with a note to Grandpa's ship saying that he knew Grandpa was there and that rather than making me walk the plank, he'd decided to keep me on board because he had a use for me.

What use?

Well, I'm in the laundry room. Turns out the other pirates hate doing Madlocks's washing as it smells AWFUL. So he's making ME do it as a punishment. My hands will stink forever. ☹

Grandpa's Proper Pirate Training never said anything about whiffy underpants.

I demand a refund.

Pirates Against Rubbish Piracy Society

The Best Pirate Ship in the World

Dead Man's Cove

The Ocean

July 22ND

Dear Tiresome, Stupid, Complete Little Idiot of a Brother,

PARPS has recently received a letter from Pirate Madlocks informing us that your pirate pet, Boris Flamebeak the ridiculous chicken, has been responsible for stealing a captain's toilet roll and insulting him.

WHAT IS THE MATTER WITH YOU??????!!!!!!!

Perhaps you are unaware that Dread Pirate Madlocks is top of our list to be the new patron of PARPS? Although I told you TWENTY TIMES last year.

Perhaps you are also unaware that, even among pirates, it is not considered "acceptable" for your pet to nick someone's toilet roll when they're using the loo! ESPECIALLY when it's DREAD PIRATE MADLOCKS! Who your big brother is trying DESPERATELY to recruit to be the new patron of parps! IN CASE YOU MISSED

IT THE FIRST TWENTY-ONE TIMES!

This is your last warning, Blunderbeard, or else I WILL come and get you . . . to personally throw you overboard to Davy Jones's Locker!

Yours sincerely, in a really bad mood with you,

Blasterous Blackbeard

(Director of PARPS)

Ah. That'll be why the name was familiar, then. Whoops. ☹

Argh! Something whizzing towards the laundry-room window!

Landed in the washing barrel and splashed dirty washing water all over my face.

Fished it out.

Cannonball wrapped in hot-pink paper.

Only one person communicates like this: Redruth. The PortaCannon™ I made for her is really accurate over long distances.

Maybe she and Grandpa have a rescue

plan! Maybe they're coming to get me – I'm saved! ☺

Oh.

Not exactly. ☹

The Breath O'Death
The Ocean

Hey, Blunders,

Yoooooooooooooooooou idiot. Boy, are you in trouble. Again. Grandpa is sooooooo not happy with you. You've gone and ruined our surprise attack! Now they know we're here, they'll be keeping an eye on Grandpa's ship! He says you'd better find another way that we can catch them off-guard. If you don't, he's going to send you back to the Island of No Return and feed you to his pet shark, Colin. That's if Madlocks doesn't get you first. Or Blackbeard. Actually, Blunders, there's quite a list. Oh, and Grandpa says don't bother trying to escape the *Laughing Skull* and swim back. He says he's not letting you on board again until we've got Madlocks's ship.

Soooooo totally glad I'm not you.

Have fun!

Laters,

R xxx

OK, OK, keep calm.

All I have to do is to work out how to save my chicken from being made into a birthday pie, come up with a plan to take over this ship which is packed with horrible pirates and hand it over to Grandpa before my hands stink for eternity. Easy. ☹

PANIC!!!!!!!!!!!!!!!

OK, deep breaths ... There must be a way out of this.

I'm sure I'll think of something. For now I'll just keep my head down ... stay out of trouble ... finish off this load of washing and—

Hang on.

Oh dear. Oh very VERY dear.

Is that a red sock in with Madlocks's white shirts?

Post. ☹

Pirates **A**gainst **R**ubbish **P**iracy **S**ociety

The Best Pirate Ship in the World

Dead Man's Cove

The Ocean

July 26th

PINK, BLUNDERBEARD?! YOU DYED ALL HIS WHITE SHIRTS PINK???!!

SORT. IT. OUT!

Yours in deepest despair at your unbelievable stupidity,

Blasterous Blackbeard

(Director of PARPS)

10am

Am now banned from doing the laundry, and have been put on dusting duty. Madlocks has a LOT of trophies.

No problem.

10.12am

Ohhhhhh dear.

I just wanted to make sure everything was really clean so I wouldn't get in trouble. Especially Madlocks's CRAZIEST HAIR OF THE YEAR AWARD. He loves that trophy.

Dusted it a bit. Knocked it off the shelf a bit. It smashed … a bit.

Now it's missing

a head.

Think I might soon be missing mine as well. ☹

I hate post.

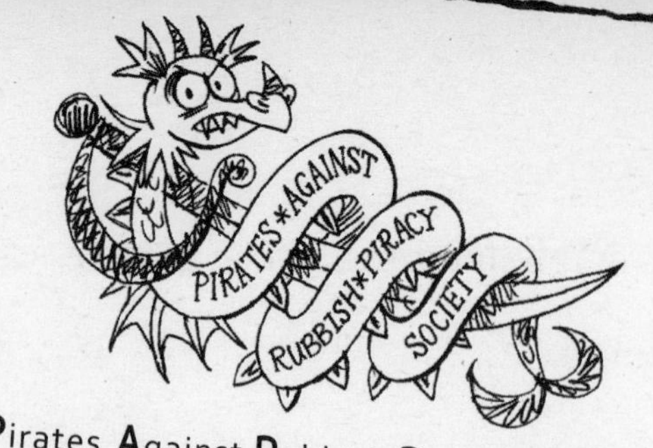

Pirates Against Rubbish Piracy Society

The Best Pirate Ship in the World

Dead Man's Cove

The Ocean

July 30th

YOU DID WHAT TO HIS TROPHY??! Do you REALLY not want Madlocks to be the patron of PARPS??!! He is FURIOUS with you. SO AM I.

Yours so very EXTREMELY crossly there aren't words I am allowed to use,

Blasterous Blackbeard

(Director of PARPS)

DIRECTOR OF PARPS

Yes. Well. Moving on. Am now on kitchen duty.

I need to:

1. Think of a plan to take over this ship.
2. Rescue doomed chicken.
3. ~~Get on with the laundry.~~
4. ~~Do the dusting.~~
5. Stay out of trouble.
6. Make pudding.

Actually, to save time, I'll be realistic:

1. Think of a plan to take over this ship.
2. Rescue doomed chicken.
3. ~~Get on with the laundry.~~
4. ~~Do the dusting.~~
5. ~~Stay out of trouble.~~ (forget it)
6. Make pudding.

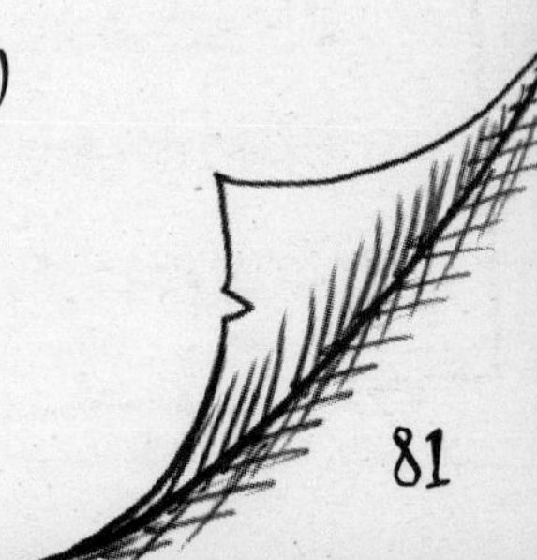

At least I'm in the kitchen now and can keep an eye on Boris. They've chained her up but are feeding her Chick-O-Snacks so that she's nice and fat for the birthday feast. She's really happy about it. She doesn't know about the pie. ☹

PLAN TO CONQUER THE LAUGHING SKULL:
OPERATION SHIP SNATCH

OPERATION SHIP SNATCH: PLAN A:
Arrange a swimming race so that all the pirates are in the water, then signal to Grandpa and Redruth to get on board and sail off with ship before they come back.

Asked Madlocks if I could send a note to Grandpa reminding him to water my cactus (sssh, pretend!).

Madlocks said no.

I said I'd bake him some lemon cupcakes.

Madlocks said yes.

He told me to give the note to one of his crew members to deliver so I chose Lazy Jim. I know Lazy Jim can't read because I saw him holding a copy of *Pirate Monthly* upside down.

This is what my note really said:

TOP SECRET

Dear Grandpa and Redruth,

I have a brilliant plan. Tomorrow I'm organising a swimming race for the crew. When you hear me blow the whistle, bring your rowing boat and we'll take over the ship. I am fine although my fingers still stink from laundry. Can't bite my nails without nearly being sick.
Boris is fine and still not a pie.

Love,
Blunderbeard

10am

Well, here we go!

Turned up on deck, wearing only my swimming trunks and a pink-swan rubber ring round my waist (it was the only one I could find).

When all the pirates stopped laughing at me (humph), they asked why I was dressed like that.

I explained that today is National Pirate Swimming Race Day – didn't they know about it? It's the latest thing.

Madlocks said of course he already knew about the race because he was the coolest pirate around – *Pirate Monthly* and *PUS* had told him so. He pretended he was waiting for the rest of the crew, and now he's gone off to get changed. All the other pirates have copied him.

I'm going to stay on deck and blow the whistle to start the race.

10.15am

They're all ready. Madlocks is wearing a swimming cap – he says his hair is too fabulous and important to get wet.

Blew the whistle.

Peered through my telescope.

Can just see Grandpa and Redruth getting into the rowing boat and heading this way.

Success will be mine.

Ohhhhhhhhhh dear.

Failure is mine.

Turns out a swimming race and angry, ferocious, giant man-eating eels don't go well together.

I'm banned from organising any sport activities ever again. On the plus side, I've

NEVER seen pirates swim that fast. Very impressive.

Peered through the telescope. Saw Grandpa and Redruth quickly rowing

back to their ship. Grandpa was waving his fist in my direction and didn't look happy.

Madlocks also ordered me to bake cupcakes for everyone to say sorry.

He's very, very cross. ☹

HOW ON THE SEVEN SEAS ARE WE GOING TO GET THIS SHIP??!!

My birthday. At least I baked a cupcake to cheer myself up.

Did I get a birthday card from my dear brother? Nope. But I did get this. ☹

Pirates Against Rubbish Piracy Society

The Best Pirate Ship in the World

Dead Man's Cove

The Ocean

August 19th

Blunderbeard,

SWIMMING RACE??!! EEL-INFESTED WATERS??!! PINK-SWAN RUBBER RING ??!! ARE YOU OUT OF YOUR TINY, TINY BRAIN?

Not only has Madlocks complained to

me AGAIN, but Captain Harry Chomp of S.M.E.L.L.S. (Society for Monsters Existing in Large Lakes and Seas) has written to me and I quote:

"Those giant man-eating eels were only released into the wild last week. The poor things are shy enough as it is without YOUR LITTLE BROTHER setting up a ridiculous swimming race to scare them to bits! Do you know how hard it is to calm down a stressed-out giant man-eating eel? Do you? I have been bitten eighty-three times and slapped round the face twice. I've had to round them all up, keep them in a huge, dark tank and feed them chamomile tea. Do you know how hard it is to persuade a giant man-eating eel

that it wants to drink chamomile tea?!

DO YOU?!"

If you don't find a way to make it up to Madlocks, I WILL NOT invite you to my birthday party (though you still have to make me that really huge, rum-flavoured birthday cupcake, because you promised).

Yours, about to explode,

Blasterous Blackbeard

(Director of PARPS)

P.S. "Happy" birthday.

Oh dear.

Maybe Blackbeard should try drinking chamomile tea in a dark tank.

2pm

Just when I thought the day couldn't get any worse:

Madlocks said he and the other pirates had had a meeting. They're fed up with me causing trouble and are making me walk the plank. I'll have to leave Boris behind and swim back to Grandpa and explain I'm a complete and utter failure. Again.

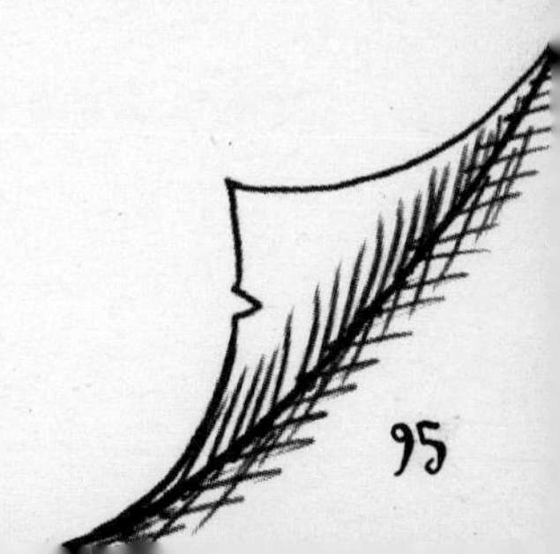

3pm

On the plank.

I'm doomed. ☹

Farewell, cruel ship. Farewell, cruel pirates. Farewell, cruel world.

4pm

Not doomed.

As I walked the plank, I told the pirates they were being especially mean as it was my birthday. No one should have to walk the plank on their birthday.

Then Madlocks said, "Shiver me timbers, boy!! I knows what ye mean! 'Tis me birthday soon and none of this rotten crew's done anything about it!"

Aha, thinks I. Maybe I won't have to walk the plank.

"You poor pirate," I said. "Instead of kicking me off your ship, why don't you let me plan your party?"

Madlocks clapped his hands together and gave a little bounce. "Deal!" he roared.

REEEEEEEEEESULT.

OPERATION SHIP SNATCH: PLAN B

And we're back on track!

Tomorrow I'm arranging for them to practise "Sleeping Sharks" for one of Madlocks's party games. So they will all lie down as quietly as they can, WITHOUT MOVING (that bit's quite important) and I'll be the one to call "Out!" if I see anyone move. The last one "in" is the winner. Except I'll trick them! I won't call anyone "out" for ages – well, not until I've lowered the flag on the ship and Grandpa and Redruth are on board and tying up the other pirates with rope.

It's a perfect plan!

10am

Sent Lazy Jim with a note to Grandpa and Redruth. Pretended it was a note asking them to renew my library book.

But really it said:

TOP SECRET

Dear Grandpa and Redruth,

Whoops.

Giant man-eating eels ... cross pirates ...

chamomile tea ... plank-walking ...

Aaaaaaaaaanyway ...

Change of plan.

When you see me lower the *Laughing Skull* flag, come across as quickly as you can.

I am well and Boris is fat.

Love,

Blunderbeard

11am

The whole crew of the *Laughing Skull* are lying face down on the deck. Being silent, still and very, very un-piratey. They are all determined to win because no pirate wants to be a loser. And because I've offered a dozen lime-and-coconut cupcakes for the winner.

11.03am

This is brilliant. The ship will be ours!

Am lowering the flag. Grandpa and Redruth will be on their way any moment.

Doing a quick (and quiet) victory dance.

Go, Blunders! Go, Blunders! Go—

11.15am

Oh no. Oh VERY no. ☹

Turns out it's rather difficult to do a quick, quiet victory dance with pirates lying all over the deck. Trod on Lazy Jim (he's very good at "Sleeping Sharks").

Wobbled.

Which made me trip over Bones.

Which made me fall backwards over Peggy Pegleg.

Which made me land SPLAT on Dread Pirate Madlocks, nearly knocking off his hat.

He was … er … shall we say, *a little bit put out*. Apparently, no one in the history of pirates has EVER DARED to touch his hat before. I can see why. He went as red as a boiled lobster from yelling so much. Wonder why he's so cross about his hat coming off? Come to think of it, I've never seen him without some sort of hat before.

Anyway, then all the pirates started arguing about who won and was going to get the cupcakes.

I quietly hoisted the flag again. Saw Grandpa and Redruth rowing back. Grandpa was jumping up and down in the boat. Glad I can't lip-read very well. ☹

Going back to the kitchen to make a dozen lime-and-coconut cupcakes for EVERYONE. ☹

New Rule: stop opening envelopes.

Pirates Against Rubbish Piracy Society

The Best Pirate Ship in the World

Dead Man's Cove

The Ocean

August 23RD

BLUNDERBEARD!

HIS HAT?! YOU TOUCHED HIS HAT?!

DO YOU NOT WANT TO LIVE ANY MORE?!

I've asked him to give you one more chance before he makes you walk the plank. ONE CHANCE, Blunderbeard, and that's it. And if he DOES make you walk the plank, I'm coming to watch.

Yours, jumping up and down on my pirate hat really crossly BECAUSE OF YOU,

Blasterous Blackbeard

(Director of PARPS)

OPERATION SHIP SNATCH: PLAN C

Get the pirates to make some birthday bunting from an old sail. When we're holding it ready to tie into place, I'll quickly spring into action and tie them all up instead! Then Grandpa and Redruth can come and storm the ship. Easy as (not chicken) pie.

Sent Lazy Jim with a note to Grandpa. Pretended I was checking if my GunkMelter™ toenail-cleaner machine is unplugged. (Haven't really invented the GunkMelter™ – well, not yet – after sharing Blackbeard's cabin a few years ago, it's DEFINITELY on the cards.)

The note really said:

TOP SECRET

Dear Grandpa and Annoying Cousin,

I've got another brilliant plan.

Bunting is my secret weapon. Who needs swords and cannons??

When you see the *Laughing Skull*'s flag lowered, please come and take over the ship.

I am well and Boris is even fatter.

Love,

Blunderbeard

Ohhhhhhhh dear.

It all started so well. They made the bunting and decorated it nicely. I lowered the flag to give Grandpa and Redruth time to get here.

I held the bunting up for everyone to see, about to spring into action with my cunning plan …

And then everything went wrong!

First, the pirates all squabbled about whose piece of bunting was prettiest.

Then they all squabbled about whose piece of bunting was biggest.

Then they all squabbled about whose piece of bunting was strongest.

I tried to stop them but was pushed out of the way, with my back against the mast. The pirates all rushed around crossly, arguing and tugging the bunting in every

direction … Left, right … round and round …

Grandpa and Redruth arrived just in time to see me tied to the mast with a piece of bunting dangling over my face.

I blew it out of the way and saw Grandpa glaring at me and Redruth taking a photo as they rowed back to their ship again. She'll probably send that photo to Blackbeard. Dratted girl! May all her freckles turn into pimples!!

OPERATION SHIP SNATCH:

PLAN D

Er …

Um … .

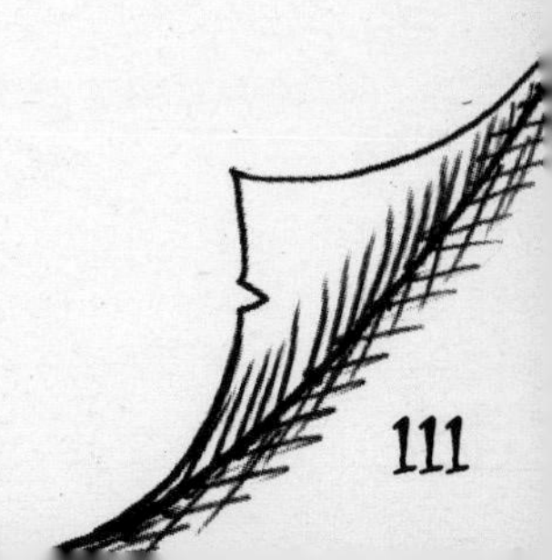

Hmm …

~~OPERATION SHIP SNATCH~~

OPERATION TOTAL DISASTER: PLAN D

Go back to Grandpa's ship, minus a fat chicken, and get forced to walk the plank.

Sorted. ☹

10am

Incoming pink cannonball!

Demolished trifle.

Splattered ship.

No pudding for hungry pirates.

And it knocked my diary into the washing-up water.

Sigh.

Now what does she want?

The Breath O'Death

The Ocean

Hey, Blunders.

Just so you know, Grandpa is getting really impatient. He says if you don't make the arrangements for us getting this ship really soon, he's soooo going to throw all your *Blunderbeard WonderWeird Contraptions* and your cake recipe books into the sea.

Suits me. I can use them for target practice.

Take your time.

Laters,

R xxx

No! Not my HenHomer™! And my PatchPolisher™! And my BeardWringer™ – I'd nearly got that to work without ripping off your beard!

And my recipe books! I had a special recipe I wanted to use for Blackbeard's stupid birthday cake and –

WAIT!

TA-DAAAHHH! Complete and utter genius-ness strikes again!

I've worked out Madlocks's weak spot – and I've had an excellent idea! Grandpa is going to be so impressed. What we need to do is distract Madlocks and his scary crew with something amazing so Grandpa and Redruth can sneak aboard, yes?

And I know just how to distract them. ☺☺☺☺☺

11am

Have offered to make Madlocks's birthday cake the biggest and best one he has <u>ever</u> had. He agreed. I said I needed my *Extra Extra Strong Baking Powder for Cakes* from Grandpa's ship.

Sent Lazy Jim with this note. It said:

TOP SECRET

Dear Grandpa and Redruth,

Plan D! I have it!

Please send over my *Extra Extra Strong Baking Powder for Cakes* with Lazy Jim.

I'm going to bake a huge, amazing cake for Madlocks. While the pirates are amazed and astounded and tucking in, we'll catch them unawares and take over the ship! Listen for me ringing the ship's bell.

I am fine and Boris is ginormous.

Love,

Blunderbeard

2pm

My diary is still soggy from the washing-up water. There are bubbles on March 10th!

Have a plan: the DiaryDryer™! This will also come in handy for whenever I accidentally drop my diary in the sea/bath/toilet.

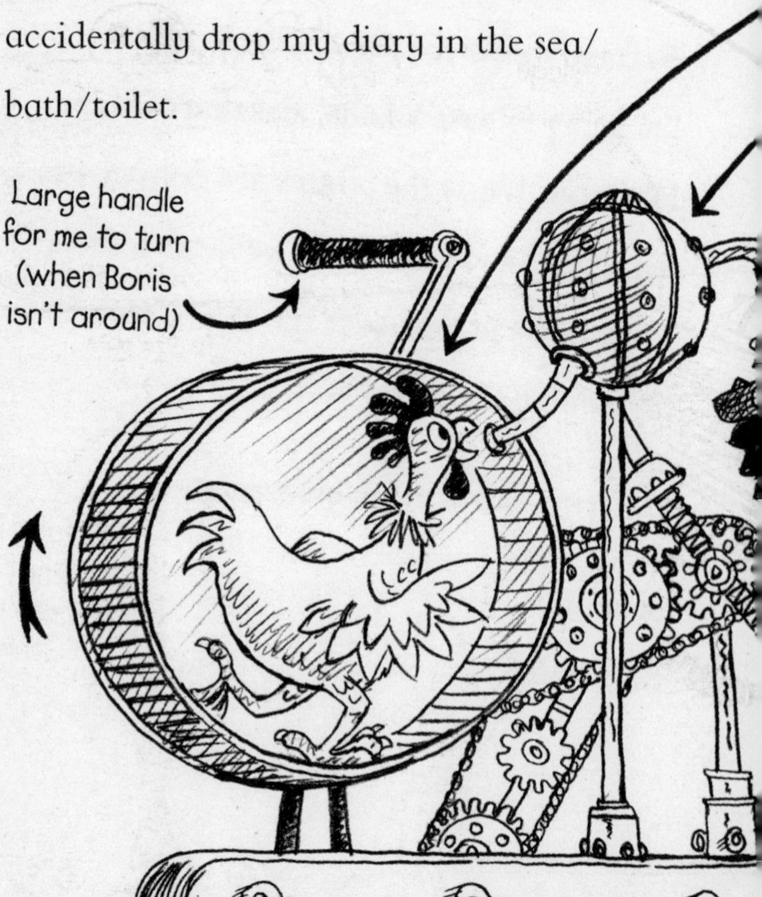

Large handle for me to turn (when Boris isn't around)

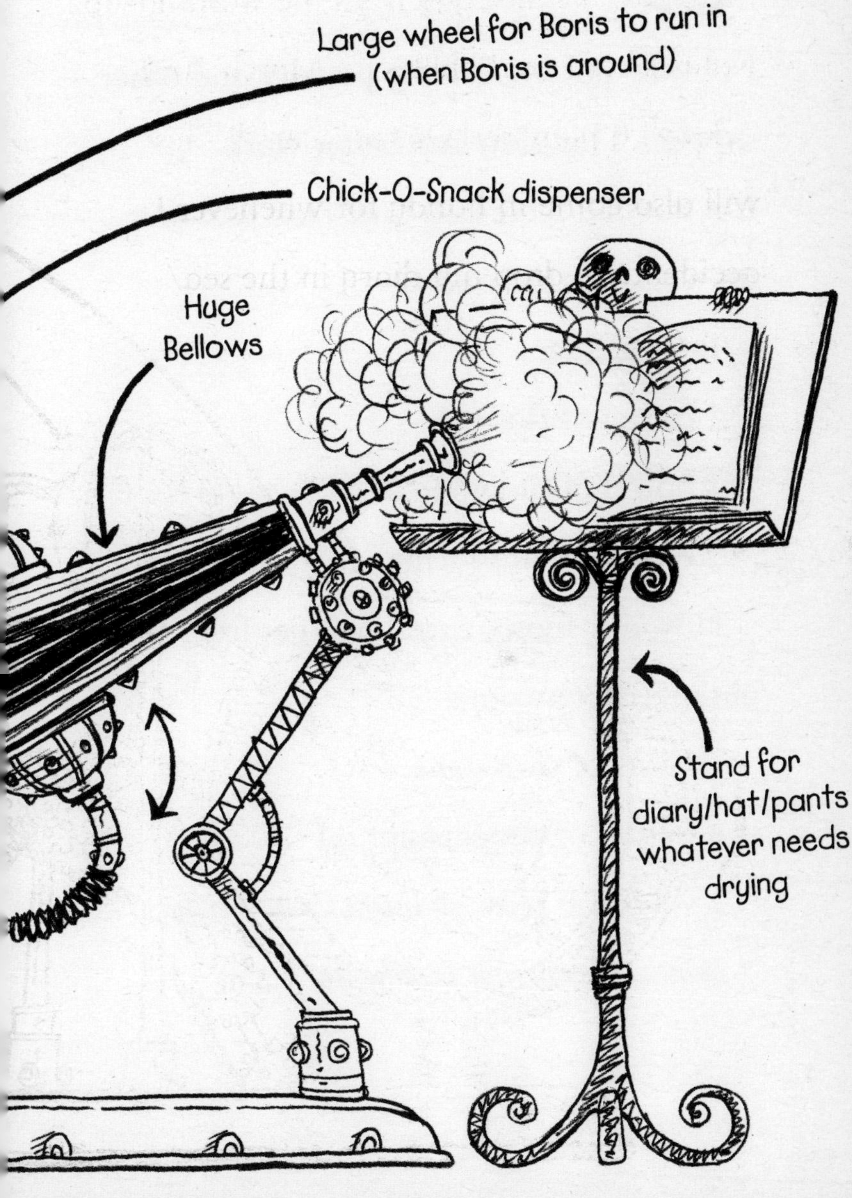

Large wheel for Boris to run in
(when Boris is around)

Chick-O-Snack dispenser

Huge
Bellows

Stand for
diary/hat/pants
whatever needs
drying

I've now got my baking powder and other supplies. This plan had better work. If it doesn't, there's no time now to come up with another one. ☹

<u>Ingredients</u>:

1 barrel of flour

1 barrel of sugar

1 barrel of margarine

However many eggs I can get from Boris in the next few days

10 bars of chocolate

4 bottles of peppermint oil

1 WHOLE JAR of *Extra Extra Strong Baking Powder for Really Big Cakes*

(Need to be careful with that. The baking powder really, REALLY doesn't mix well with fire and was the reason my ship sank last year, through no fault of my own. Anyway … more later. I need to make a birthday cake!)

10am

Baking.

2pm

Still baking.

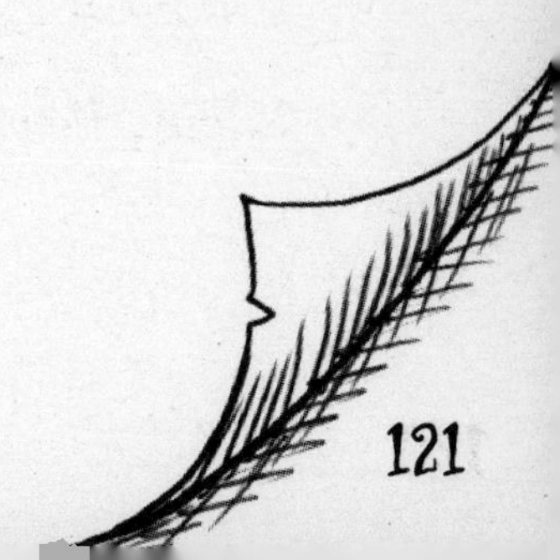

4pm

Fed up with baking. Pleeeeeeeeeeeeeeease let my plan work.

7pm

Decorating the biggest, most amazing, mint chocolate birthday cake the world has ever seen. This, ladies and gentlemen, is our secret weapon. Barnacles Blunderbeard will conquer the ship of the Dread Pirate Madlocks ... with a cake!

9am

Madlocks's birthday!

Time to put my magnificent plan into action.

This will be great. They're going to be so amazed by the cake, and all stuffing their faces so they won't even notice Grandpa and Redruth boarding the ship.

What could possibly go wrong?

Actually … let's not go there.

Still something's nagging at the back of my mind like a great, big … nagging thing.

What have I forgotten?

10am

PARTY TIME!!

Madlocks said he's spent three hours getting his hair to look just perfect for the party! (And I thought Redruth was bad.)

The pirates wanted to play "Musical Thumps". So when the accordion stops … you thump the nearest pirate before they thump you. I'm making them stop because Bones has been bopped on the nose and started to cry.

Perhaps a nice, quiet game of "Pin the Hook on the Pirate".

10.15am

Nope! Bad idea.

Just unpinning Lazy Jim from the mast …

11am

Time to do the treasure hunt. I've hidden some little chocolate gold coins all over the ship. Surely that should keep them out of trouble for five minutes.

11.15am

For the love of cupcakes! Whenever anyone found any "treasure", all the pirates fought to claim it for themselves!!

Had to get very firm with the crew. Have now made everyone sit down in a circle with their arms folded, their legs crossed and their fingers on their lips.

I've said they have to be quiet and behave themselves for ONE MINUTE (one minute – that's all I ask!) and *then* they can play pass the parcel.

11.16am

Making them stay quiet for another minute because they all giggled when Peggy Pegleg belched.

11.17am

Right. NOW we can play pass the parcel.

I'm playing the accordion and they can

open a layer of the parcel when I stop.

Simple, right?

11.23am

… Unless the parcel stops RIGHT between two pirates, and they can't agree which one should get it.

Massive swordfight … four pirates overboard … and somehow the parcel got loaded into a cannon and fired out into the middle of the sea.

Where it was gobbled up by a giant man-eating (and parcel-eating) eel.

Guess Captain Chomp has let them out again. Don't suppose he'll be pleased to discover one's just eaten a musical telescope.

12pm

Party food! Thank goodness! Should be harder for them to yell and squabble with their mouths full of food.

12.05pm

OK, make that "party-food fight".

Am ducking the tuna sandwiches and prawn cocktail crisps flying across the table.

AAAARGH! Madlocks just threw orange squash all over Peggy Pegleg and got my diary wet too! Not happy!!!!!!

Have now taken DiaryDryer™ on deck to dry diary after I've served cake (humph). And now for the giant birthday cake!!!

Just poking the candles in. It looks delicious.

About to carry it up to the deck now. Here we go!

I can see Grandpa and Redruth! They've tucked their rowing boat next to the *Laughing Skull*. Redruth has her PortaCannon™ and Grandpa has his trusty sword.

What do I have? An oversized cake and a fat chicken chained up in a kitchen.

Grandpa and Redruth are ready to storm the ship.

My heart's thumping.

This had better work.

If only I could remember that thing I've forgotten … .

Right, lighting the candles NOW.

Clearing my throat, ready to sing.

"Happy birthday to you ..." all the pirates have stopped throwing the crab pies and are joining in. Excellent. I have their attention. Any moment now, Grandpa and Redruth will spring into action ...

WAIT! The thing bugging me at the back of my mind!

The *Extra Extra Strong Baking Powder* ... explosive ... blew up my ship ... keep away from fire ...

CANDLES!!!!!!!!!

OH NO – I'm going to blow up the ship!

Must knock cake overboard!

AAAAAAAAAARGH!!!!!

BOOM.

It exploded in mid-air – cake is flying everywhere!

Madlocks says he loves the fireworks!

Now all the pirates are scrambling to get the cake!

Right – this is it! Ringing the bell! Getting a few odd looks.

Now singing "Happy Birthday" as I ring the bell. They seem very pleased with that and are stuffing more cake into their mouths.

Grandpa and Redruth are aboard.

The fight for the ship is on!

12.20pm

Redruth's PortaCannon™ is going off somewhere – hats flying in all directions. Can hear her whooping. Sounds like she's having a great time.

Grandpa is fighting about three of Madlocks's crew – oh, and managing to eat cake and cartwheel at the same time. I should probably help him … but, well … fighting has never been my strong point. And everything looks under control here … If "control" is utter, utter chaos. Time to find Boris.

Let "Operation Big Bird" begin!

12.25pm

Trying to dodge the barrels which are crashing across the decks. Can hear Grandpa cheering. Don't think he's had this much fun in ages.

In the kitchen. There's Boris the Huge!

Good grief. She looks like a feathery football with legs.

Sorry, Madlocks, chicken pie's off the menu!

Come on, Boris – pull at the chains!

She's just looking at me and burping. She'd rather sit here getting fed and getting fat.

PULL AT THE CHAINS, BORIS!

Oh. That. CHICKEN!

AHA! The pirates have left the Chick-O-Snacks on the table. All I need to do is leave a little trail of them. She's straining to reach them. Anything for Chick-O-Snacks! She's pulling and yanking …

She's snapped the chains!

Right, grabbed Boris – now back up to find Grandpa and Redruth.

12.28am

YEEK!

All the pirates are fighting each other now! I think they've forgotten who or what they were fighting about in the first place and are just having a jolly good time.

Just heard Madlocks bellow that this is the best birthday party he's ever had and he loves the "party entertainment".

TRIPLE YEEK! Redruth just blew Grandpa's hat off! No pudding for her tonight, then.

Boris? Boris, what are you doing?

COME BACK!

She's running through the crowd … she's … she's seen my DiaryDryer™! She's climbing in! She must have sniffed out the Chick-O-Snacks!

She's gobbling loads of Chick-O-Snacks! She's in overdrive! Boris! Slow down!

She's blowing up a mighty breeze! Everyone's stopped to find out where the breeze is coming from. The last remaining hats are tumbling overboard, except Madlocks's. He's clinging to his like mad.

OH NO! Here comes Madlocks, marching towards us. WE'VE HAD IT!

Hang on, I've got an idea. He really doesn't want his hat to come off, does he?

Why not? What's he hiding? Let's find out!!

QUICK! Turning dial to HURRICANE TURBO setting. Pointing it right at Madlocks!

AAARGH! Strong – wind!

Madlocks – yelling.

Am – clinging –

to – mast.

Madlocks's hat – blown off! – and now – hair blown off! – was wig! – now bald head!

Everyone gasping – Redruth giggling.

Tattoo on head – "I LOVE MUMMY".

Phew! The breeze has stopped. Boris is so stuffed, she's fallen asleep.

Everyone staring at Madlocks.

ABSOLUTE STUNNED SILENCE ON DECK. (Until Boris starts snoring.)

No more winning Barber Rossa's Craziest Hair Awards for him.

Now's my big moment. I know JUST what to do to save the day.

Ready.

Steady.

GO!

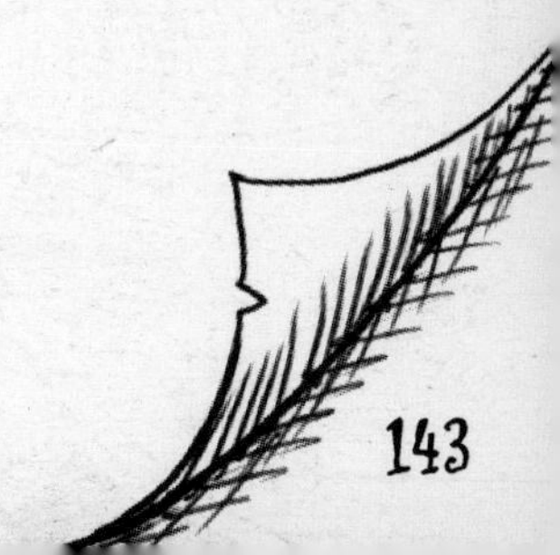

5pm

So, what happened?

Well, it was my big moment. I remembered all of Grandpa's Proper Pirate Training and decided I'd better make an entrance. I grabbed one of the ropes and started swinging.

I was aiming to land in the crow's nest. I missed, swung across the deck and knocked over two pirates. Then the rope twisted round the mast, and I swung into it head-first with an almighty WALLOP and fell to the ground in a heap. Ow. My. Head.

Everyone was watching me. So I got dizzily to my feet and wobbled over to Madlocks.

"Madlocks, Grandpa is writing *Proper Pirating for Beginners: Volume 3*," I said, as the ship began to spin around me.

The pirates all went "ooh" and gave Grandpa the thumbs-up. Oh. Grandpa has a fan club.

"AND," I continued, seeing double everywhere, "he will write your entry and tell EVERYONE about your tattoo and that your hair isn't real."

The pirates all went "ooh" again.

"That is, unless you give this ship back to Grandpa," I said, wondering why Madlocks had grown two heads. "You took it from him and he wants it back NOW."

Actually, Blunders, you were getting really dizzy from the bump on your head by then. That might be what you **MEANT** to say. Kinda came out "You. Ship. Grandpa. Two heads! Two heads! NOW." and then you passed out.

Shut up, Redruth, this is my story, OK? Get out of my diary and find me an ice pack or something helpful.

Idiot.

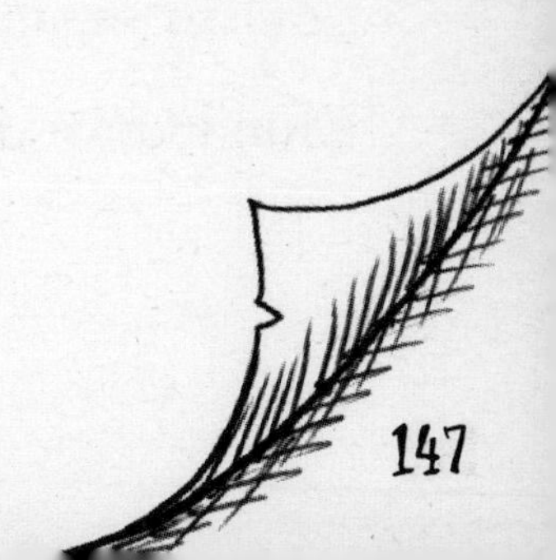

OK, so if anyone asks how I got the big bump on my head, I'll mention fighting Madlocks, and maybe just skip the details. The point is – we GOT THE SHIP! Madlocks blamed Bones for not ordering the special wig glue in time and said Bones had to get him a really good birthday present to make up for it. Like a new ship.

We left them all on Doom Island. Madlocks was really cross but I still think he had a birthday to remember. And we let them take the rest of the birthday cake. We are now sailing the *Breath O'Death* and the *Laughing Skull* back to Dead Man's Cove as I write. Grandpa was really proud and said I'd finally learned a thing or two about pirating.

Sort of…

Grandpa is taking us back to Dead Man's Cove in time for a family Christmas, but he won't stay. He says he needs some time to write *Proper Pirating for Beginners: Volume 3* now.

And recover from having us on board for a year.

He'll keep in touch though, and pop in from time to time. It'll be odd going back to Dead Man's Cove, but I'm sure another adventure will turn up.

Back in Dead Man's Cove.

Christmas was "interesting", especially when Boris decided to be the fairy on top of the tree.

Mum gave me a new hat and Blackbeard gave me a new bottle of ChickaPoo. Grumph.

And Redruth stuck this note in my diary:

Hey Blunders!

Thought you'd like to hear the good news. As Dad's busy looking after the treasure on the Island of No Return, your mum said I can stay with you. Bet you're sooooo pleased.

This is gonna be fun!!

Laters,

R xxx

Well, THAT will be something to look forward to.

Time to think about my New Year's resolutions. This year, for the first time EVER, I don't have to think about stopping biting my nails. (Yuck. I'm never doing that again!!)

So here are my resolutions:

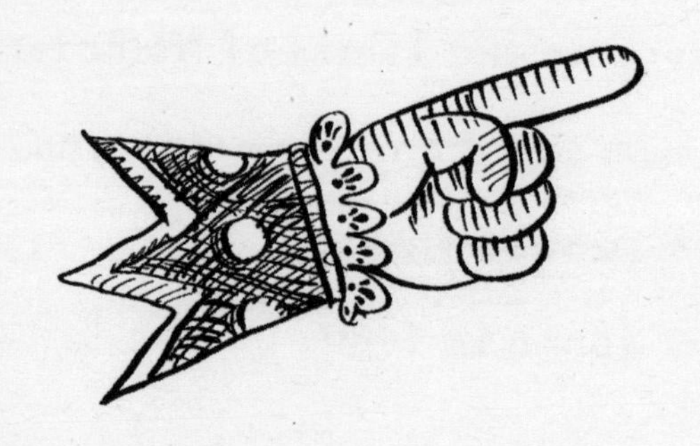

1. Prove to my big brother Blackbeard once and for all that I am NOT a waste of space.
2. Teach Boris a special new skill.
3. Do something awesome and make it into *Pirate Monthly* - well, why not?
4. Find a way to get rid of Redruth.

Wish me luck! ☺

THE END

Don't miss Pirate Blunderbeard and Boris's first adventure . . .

Dare you join Pirate Blunderbeard and Boris on the Island of No Return?

Coming Soon

WORST. MOVIE. EVER.